Jamie was born in Wales but now lives in Scotland. Jamie's writing is inspired by the love of reading with his daughters. The idea for the character Star came from the name of Jamie's second daughter, Seren, which in the Welsh language means 'star'.

THE STAR FROM AFAR

JAMIE MORRIS

AUSTIN MACAULEY PUBLISHERS™
LONDON ★ CAMBRIDGE ★ NEW YORK ★ SHARJAH

Copyright © Jamie Morris (2021)

A CIP catalogue record for this title is available from the British Library.

ISBN 9781398453531 (Paperback)
ISBN 9781398453548 (Hardback)
ISBN 9781398453562 (ePub e-book)

www.austinmacauley.com

First Published (2021)
Austin Macauley Publishers Ltd
25 Canada Square
Canary Wharf
London
E14 5LQ

For Seren and Beth, my stars

The Star from afar had a strange dream one night,
You're needed on Earth, a world out of sight.

Excited, she got up and packed a red case,
With a toothbrush she's leaving on a long trip
through space.

100,000Lyrs

A galaxy to travel, but does she know the way?
Our star begins her journey – 100,000 light years away.

An alien with three eyes and a nose that's cherry red,
Two feet, two arms and purple hair, sprouting from his head.

'Miss Star, I'm glad I met you here, my ship won't start, it broke,
It's too dark in the engine room, to fix things there's no hope.'

'Tell me how to help,' said Star, 'I'll do everything I can.'
'Shine bright outside my spaceship and I'll fix the broken fan.'
Star lights up the window, her rays shine bright and true,
A bang bang here, a twist just there, the fan turns.
'Oh thank you.'

75,000 Lyrs

'Why thank you Star for helping me,
to you I give this gift.
A map of space and a length of rope,
hold tight I'll give a lift.'

A galaxy to travel, a map to guide the way,
With the alien's lift, a good head start – 75,000 light years away.

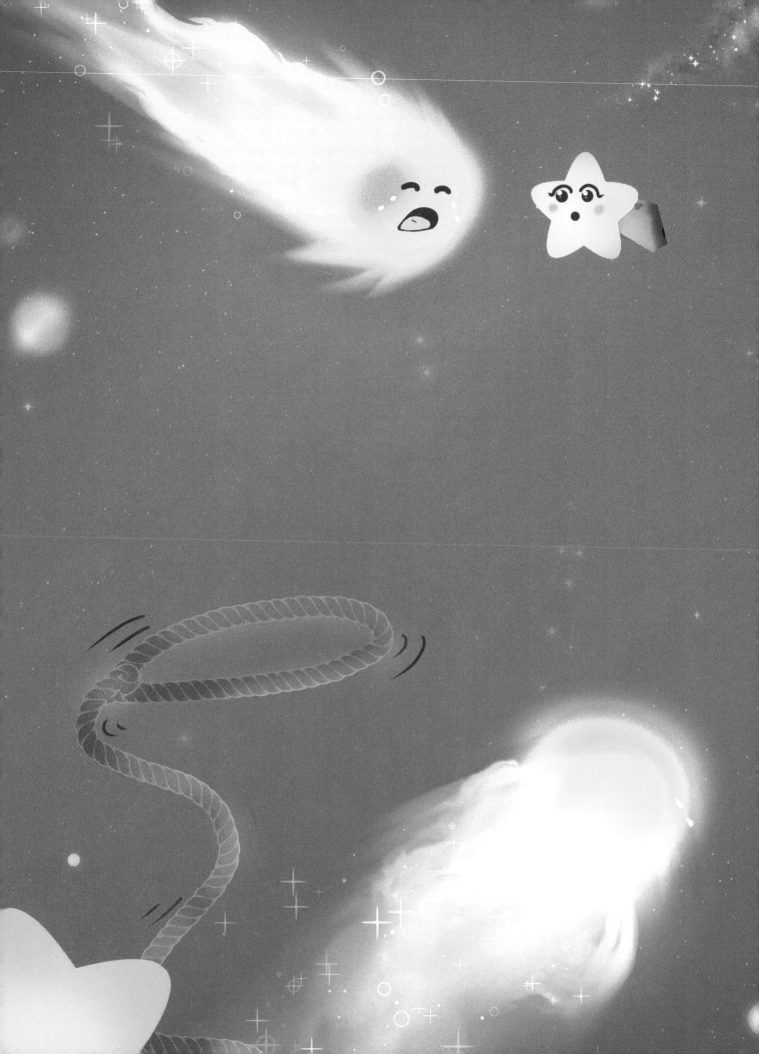

A comet flashed in front of Star and shouted, 'Help at last!
Oh Star, oh Star, please slow me down, I'm travelling too fast.'
Hot fire flaming from behind, sparks shooting all around.
'What can I do, now let me think.' Guess what Star had found?

The rope the alien gave her, a piece both thick and strong,
Our Star, she made a loop in it and threw it far and long.
It caught around the comet's tail, the edge began to fray,
Star held tight, pulled the comet back, she slowed, she
stopped, hooray!

50,000 Lyrs

'Why thank you Star for helping me, you really
are a friend,
Take this clock to tell the time, when you're
near your journey's end.'

A galaxy to travel, Star continues on her way
A ticking clock, it's still night-time – 50,000
light years away.

A crying sun, just
sitting there,
looking very sad,
A tear running down her face,
I hope it's nothing bad.
'Every time I go to bed,
every night I'm yawning,
I sleep so long, so long in fact,
I rise late every morning.'

Children being late for school,
milkmen in their beds,
Cockerels sing "cock a
doodle doo", still locked up in
their sheds.

25,000 Lyrs

The clock the comet gave her, a clock that starts to shake,
An alarm that's set for sunrise, the sun is wide awake.

'Why thank you Star for helping me, your journey's nearly done,
Keep heading to the Planet Earth, you'll know why you're
the one.'

A galaxy to travel, our Star can see the way,
Her task is set, her role awaits – 25,000 light years away.

Three kings on camels, travelling,
the road has far to go,
It's getting dark, the trail has gone, the kings are lost, you know.

Our Star shines brightly up above and says, 'I'll show the way,
I'll lead you all to Bethlehem and the very first Christmas Day.'

In a stable, behind the Inn, a donkey, shepherds, and sheep,
Join Mary, Joseph, two brown cows and a new-born baby asleep.

The kings arrive, with gifts they bring,
of frankincense, myrrh and gold,
They lay them down, the baby smiles,
the Nativity tale is told.

Why thank you Star for helping us,
your journey finally ends,
Three Kings, an alien, a comet, a sun
are all your new found friends.

A galaxy's been travelled, our Star is
here to stay,
No miles left to travel, no more light
years away.

Now every night on Christmas Eve, be sure to look up high,
The brightest star that you can see is our Star in the sky.

CPSIA information can be obtained
at www.ICGtesting.com
Printed in the USA
BVHW051208010621
608554BV00007B/1003